Jeffery Deaver

The Deliveryman: A Lincoln Rhyme Short Story

I

Thursday, 8:30 p.m.

What's the story, Sachs? How was the scene? Complicated? Difficult? *Impossible?*"

Lincoln Rhyme turned his motorized wheelchair from his computer, where he'd been reading an email, toward the arched doorway of his parlor.

Amelia Sachs was walking into his parlor-*cum*-laboratory on Central Park West. She deposited on a nearby evidence table the large gray milk crate she was lugging, then pulled off her black 511 tactical jacket. She was clothed in blue jeans and a T-shirt — off-white today — that were typical of what she wore beneath the Tyvek overalls when she walked the grid at a crime scene. Her pretty face, her former fashion model face, eased into a smile. "The scene? Challenging, let's say. You're in a good mood."

"He is. It's pretty disorienting." This came from Rhyme's aide just entering the room behind Sachs. Thom Reston, a slim young man, was impeccably dressed in dark gray Italian slacks and a solid taupe shirt. Rhyme was a quadriplegic — his spine damaged at the C4 level — and largely paralyzed from the neck down. Accordingly, and not surprisingly, he was given to swings of temperament that could be quite dramatic. (Of course, even before the accident that rendered him disabled, as head of the NYPD crime scene operation, he'd been dour to insufferable quite often, he'd been fast to admit.) Thom was in a good position to voice an opinion on the matter; after years of caregiving, he knew his charge's emotional gravity quite well, the way one half of a long-married couple knows the other's by instinct.

"My moods are hardly relevant. Why would they be?" His eyes were on the crate — containing evidence from the complicated, difficult and, if not impossible, then challenging homicide scene Sachs had just run in Manhattan.

Sachs seemed amused by the half-hearted denial. She asked, "The Baxter case?"

"If I were in a good mood — though again, irrelevant — that *might* be a source."

The Baxter prosecution had been a particularly tough one, unique for Rhyme; he could not recall handling another purely white collar criminal case in his years as an NYPD detective or, more recently, a forensic consultant. Baxter, an Upper Eastsider/Long Islander, had been charged with scamming millions from other Upper Eastsider/Long Islanders (true, the vics came from all over the New York metro area but were all of the same pedigree). Most could probably afford to lose the money but, wherever your socialist or income inequality sympathies lay, one cannot take what belongs to others. The former stockbroker and bond trader devised exceedingly clever financial scams that had hummed away, undetected, for several years. An assistant DA had discovered the schemes, though, and she'd asked Rhyme to assist on the evidentiary side of the case. He'd had to bring all his forensic skills to the game to identify cash trails, drop sites, remote locations from which pay phone and other landline calls were made, meetings in restaurants and bars and state parks, physical presence on private jets, relevant documents and *objets d'art* purchased with stolen cash.

Rhyme had managed to pull together enough evidence for a conviction on wire fraud and larceny and other financial offenses but, not content with those crimes alone, he kept digging... and found that Baxter was more of a threat than it seemed at first glance. Rhyme had found evidence that he'd participated in at least one shooting and discovered an illegal pistol hidden in a self-storage unit. The detectives and DA couldn't find any physical victims; it was speculated that he'd simply intimidated some poor mark with a well-placed .45 shot or two. The absence of a bullet-riddled victim, though, was irrelevant; possessing a handgun without proper license was a serious felony. The DA added the charge and, just today, the jury returned a guilty-on-all-counts verdict.

Lincoln Rhyme lived for the — okay—*challenge* of forensic work and once his contribution to a case was finished, he grew uninterested. Today, however, the ADA had just sent Rhyme an email in which she reported the verdict while adding a footnote: One of the victims scammed by Baxter out of her nest egg had tearfully thanked the prosecutor and "anyone else who helped in the trial." The guilty verdict meant she would have a much easier path in suing Baxter to recoup some of the stolen funds. She'd be able to send her grandchildren to college, after all.

Rhyme regarded sentiment as perhaps the least useful of emotions, yet he was pleased at his contribution to *People v. Baxter*. Hence the, yes, good mood.

But Baxter was going into the system, Rhyme's role was over and so: Time to get back to work. He inquired once more about the homicide scene Sachs had just run in Manhattan.

She responded, "Victim was thirty-eight-year-old Eduardo 'Echi' Rinaldo, worked as a deliveryman. Had his own company, legit. But he also did a little street dealing — grass and coke mostly — and transported whatever the crews needed moved, which was a little *less than* legit: stolen merch, drugs, even undocumenteds."

"Bodies?"

"That's right. Well, live ones." She shrugged. "He was freelance, worked for anybody who paid, but mostly the Latino crews. GT had next to nothing on him."

The Organized Crime Division's Gang Taskforce, operating out of NYPD headquarters at One Police Plaza, was unequaled in tracking crews in the metro area. If GT didn't have info on the late Echi he was insignificant indeed.

"So gangs've taken to outsourcing," he mused.

"Why pay benefits and retirement plans, you can avoid it?" She smiled and continued, "He was slashed to death in an alley and I mean *slashed*. Don't have the weapon but I'd say serrated blade. Jugular, wrists. He tried to crawl to the street but didn't get very far. Bled out, ME says, in two, three minutes."

The perp must've known what he was doing. The vast majority of stab wounds are superficial, and quick death from a sharpened edge requires attention to important veins and arteries.

Rhyme's eyes had turned to the milk crate she'd brought in. "That's all you collected?"

The doorbell sounded and Thom went to answer it. Rhyme noticed Sachs give a faint — and, it seemed to him, wry — laugh.

He saw why a moment later. Two ECTs walked into the lab wheeling hand trucks on which were bungeed a dozen milk crates similar to the one Sachs had just carried in by herself. Each crate was filled to overflowing.

"Ask and ye shall receive," Sachs said.

"That's from *one* scene?" Rhyme asked.

"You wanted impossible."

"Not *that* impossible."

She'd collected, by his count, perhaps five hundred items of evidence from the Rinaldo killing. As every criminalist knew, too much evidence was as troublesome as not enough.

She said, "We've got cigarette butts, roach clips, food wrappers, coffee cups, a kid's toy, beer cans, broken bottles, condoms, scraps of paper, receipts. It was one messy alley."

"Jesus."

Sachs greeted the evidence collection techs — both women, Latina and Anglo — and directed them to place what they'd brought on examination tables. The darker-skinned woman cast a worshipful gaze toward Rhyme. Not many evidence collection techs — entry level at CSU — got a glimpse of the legendary criminalist.

Rhyme gave a neutral tip of the head; he had as little need for reverence as he did for sentiment, probably less.

Sachs, however, thanked them and referred to some social get-together with one or both or someone else that was in the works and they left.

Her phone hummed and she took a call, stepped aside to speak for a moment. Her face was grim. Rhyme deduced, though he wasn't certain, that the call was personal. Her mother had been having serious health issues lately — cardiac surgery loomed — and Sachs, both his professional and romantic partner, had been preoccupied with the woman's condition lately.

She disconnected. He glanced at her and received a noncommittal shake of the head in response. Meaning: Later. Now, the case. Let's move on.

He said to her, "Rinaldo? The details?"

"He was driving a panel truck, a sixteen footer. Six p.m. he parked outside a bodega on West Three-one, for cigarettes. When he came out there was some altercation. Not sure what, exactly. Argument. Shouting. The witness couldn't hear the words."

"Witness." This didn't encourage Rhyme much. He believed in the cold science of evidence and deeply distrusted accounts of those present at a crime, whether participants or observers.

"His son. Eight years old. He was in the truck, waiting."

"So he saw it happen." Rhyme could reluctantly accept that an *eyewitness* to the actual incident might make some contributions to investigators — if they remained suitably skeptical.

But Sachs said, "No. The killing happened in the back of an alley beside the store. The boy never got out of the cab of the truck. He says he saw a form — a man, he thinks, in a hat, but no other ID — run from the alley into the street, *behind* the truck. He flagged a cab. The boy said it was a regular car that pulled over. So, a gypsy."

"Any leads?"

"Not so far. Some detectives're canvassing but I don't hope for much more."

Gypsy, or unlicensed, taxi companies kept few records and the owners and drivers were reluctant to assist the police, since they operated just below the surface of the law. "But the boy — his name is Javier — thinks he heard the perp tell the driver 'the Village.' He didn't hear anything else. Then the car took off."

Greenwich Village embraced many blocks and hundreds of acres. Without more to narrow down his destination, the killer might have said "Connecticut." Or "New England."

"Funny, though," Sachs said, "with Rinaldo's job — deliveryman for the crews? What was the perp's connection with the Village?"

The colorful and quirky neighborhood was not — had never been — known for gang activity. Although the Village had been settled largely by Italian immigrants, the organized crime families did not live or work there; they were centered in Little Italy — south of the East Village — and in Brooklyn and, to some extent, the Bronx. Today the only "underworld" crew living on Bleecker and Greenwich and West Fourth worked on Wall Street and represented too-big-to-fail-whatever-nonsense-we-get-up-to banks and brokerage houses.

Rhyme glanced at the evidence bags and jars Sachs had collected. The items inside might possibly tell them something about where exactly in the Village they had gone — if in fact he had a professional or personal connection with the place and wasn't just after a trendy meal or mixologist's signature cocktail; even murderers read the Wednesday food section of the *New York Times*.

"Not a hijacking or robbery?"

"No. The padlock on the back of the truck was intact, and the key was still in Rinaldo's pocket. And his wallet and cash — a few hundred — weren't touched. If he had anything else with him, why would the perp take that and leave the money?"

"Anything inside the truck?"

"No, empty. And there was no manifest or delivery schedule. Whatever he was supposed to deliver that day got delivered. The bodega clerk — who didn't see the perp, he claims — says there was another witness, a woman across the street. But I couldn't find her. Canvassing for her too."

"Where the hell is Mel Cooper?" Rhyme grumbled. He'd called the evidence technician to come in and assist in the analysis. That had been a half hour ago and though Cooper had said it would take him sixty minutes or so to arrive Rhyme's impatience was swelling.

Sachs didn't bother to respond. She pinned her hair up and stuffed it under a surgical bonnet. Then she pulled on latex gloves, goggles and face mask. She ordered the evidence according to, Rhyme instructed, the location where it had been collected at the scene.

My, there *was* a lot of it.

As she sorted the items she said, "Javier. He was pretty upset."

"Who?"

"The son, Rinaldo's son."

"Sure. Guess he would be." Rhyme asked absently, "He's with his mother?"

"No mother." She may have smiled — he couldn't tell with the mask — as she added, "I asked him if he had a mother. He said, 'Everybody's got a mother.' Then he said she'd left years ago. I got him to Child and Family Services for tonight. Tomorrow he'll go into emergency foster care. I said I'd take him."

"Why?"

"Because I wanted to. There's an aunt somewhere he hasn't seen in years but he remembers her and liked her. CFS is looking. But no hurry. I don't want him with relatives until we find out more about what dad was up to and who took him out. And the perp himself might think he was more of a witness than he was."

She stood back, beside Rhyme, and, with hands on her slim hips, regarded the evidence.

"My sense is it was just random. Not a professional hit."

Rhyme supposed he agreed. But he wasn't much interested in the line of inquiry that sought to answer *why* someone was killed. The motive underlying a crime was far less important to him than the physical consequences produced by it. That is, the evidence.

Which he wheeled forward to examine now.

II

Friday, 9 a.m.

The delivery had been shipped without problem. It had avoided detection by Customs, Immigration, Border Patrol, Coast Guard, FBI, Interstate Commerce Commission weigh stations... even state police, and local speed trap cops.

It had arrived in the borough of Manhattan.

But then...

The glitch.

And a major one it was.

The delivery was missing. The delivery he had spent $487,000 for (currency exchange issues, otherwise the purchase price would have been an even half million).

This cool spring morning Miguel Ángel Morales sat in his brownstone, on East 127th Street. He owned the whole building — and those on either side as well, as much for security as for rental income. Well, *more* for security; a wealthy man, he was more worried about losing his life, or those of his wife and sons, than his money. Morales ran the 128 Lords, a nondenominational crew numbering about fifty strong in Spanish Harlem. It was a blend of Mexican (the majority), Honduran and Guatemalan, some papered, some not. Whites too. They could be helpful — for instance, if you didn't want your man stop-and-frisked while out on a job, even though the cops weren't doing that any more, absolutely not. Civil liberties rule. Hilarious thought.

Anglos were as far as Morales's open arms extended, however, and Jamaicans, Cubans, Colombians, blacks, Chinese, Vietnamese could apply elsewhere.

The handsome man, compact and strong, sat by the window and looked out over the dark street, sipping coffee (Cubano — he was happy to embrace the food and culture from what he believed to be an overly self-important island, if not the people themselves). The brew, sticky and sweet, tickling the intersection of upper and lower jaw, normally brought him comfort. Now it did nothing.

His buy money was gone. And his deliveryman had not delivered. He waited at the agreed meeting place, no show. He'd called the man's burner five times — the maximum he allowed — and when there was no answer, he threw his Nokia out and left the restaurant fast. Just because you didn't buy a phone with a credit card didn't mean it was untraceable. At forty-five, Morales was not as tech savvy as some in his crew — or even his ten-year-old twins — but he was well aware of pings and cellular towers.

"Miguel Ángel?" His wife of eighteen years stepped into the doorway of his study.

The room, dark and quiet, was Morales's and his only. He ran his crew from a social club a block north. This was his private place. And although she was helpful in running his crew and a powerful, and dangerous, woman in her own right, she waited until he gestured her in. Which he now did.

Connie was more Anglo than he, by blood, and had a light complexion and brown hair (his was jet black, though some of the shade came from a bottle). She had a voluptuous figure, which never failed to appeal even after all these years of marriage. Now, though, he merely took in her concerned face and turned back to the window.

"Still nothing?" she asked.

She knew of the problem.

"No word." A nod, indicating the whole of the New York City area. "It's out there somewhere. But it might as well be on Mars."

"You need something?"

He shook his head. She returned to the kitchen. She was baking — a process that was a mystery to Miguel Ángel Morales. He'd never cooked a single thing in his life. Oh, he appreciated the processes involved: chemistry and heat. But he employed them in a slightly different way: an acid attack on a rival last year and burning to death an interloper from the Bronx (he could still summon the unpleasant scent of burnt skin and hair).

This morning his wife was baking coffee cakes. The smells were orange and cinnamon.

Morales sipped coffee, then set down the tiny cup, painted with pictures of blank-faced birds. Chickens, he supposed. They were yellow, their beaks blood red.

He was regarding the street before him — brownstones similar to his, women going to stores, returning from stores, boys playing soccer, even though this was a school day.

His phone hummed. Today's burner, good for another ten or twelve hours.

The caller was Morales's main lieutenant.

"Yes?" Please let there be good news.

Four hundred eighty-seven thousand dollars...

"I just found out why our deliveryman didn't show. He's dead. Got knifed in Midtown."

"*What?* Who did it?"

"No idea. Never heard Rinaldo was at risk."

"I didn't either. Wouldn't have used him if he had been."

Echi Rinaldo worked freelance for a lot of crews. He had no territory of his own and no allegiance, except to ply his trade of getting "difficult shipments" (the term the wiry man used with some humor) into the hands of purchasers or borrowers. He never cheated anyone and kept his mouth shut.

"We know," the man continued, "that he hid the delivery without any problem."

"You think this man, this killer, followed him and tortured him to find out where it was?"

"Unlikely. From what I've heard it was a street fight. He died in a few minutes. And more or less in public. You want me to find who did it and—"

"I'm not interested, at this point," Morales said calmly, "in that. Finding the delivery: That's our only mission."

A pause on the other end of the line. "The seller has the money."

"That's not an issue either." The seller would not take Morales's money and steal back the delivery. Morales knew the man's operation well. That double-dipping would serve little purpose. Besides, the relationship between them was a partnership, and it was far too early in the game for one partner to screw the other. "What else do you know?"

"We're monitoring scanners. Nobody has much info. Wasn't a hijacking and there were no contracts out on anybody fitting his description."

"Use who you need to — but only our men, or people deep in our pocket — and find out what you can, retrace Rinaldo's steps, get surveillance in place on anyone who knows anything. Police too if you need to."

"Yessir. Oh, one more thing."

"Yes?"

"Rinaldo wasn't alone when it happened. He had his son with him."

Ah, yes. That's right. Morales recalled this. It was decided that he'd take the boy with him on his rounds yesterday to give an air of innocence if he were stopped for a traffic violation. He'd never met the boy but believed him to be about eight or nine.

"What did he see?"

"Nothing, from what we're picking up on the chatter. But who knows?"

"I'll keep that in mind. Now, get started."

"Yessir."

He disconnected and, his jaw tight, looked over the soccer players. They *should* be in school. Where were their parents?

He reflected on his lieutenant's call and decided this was not the time to save fifty-nine dollars. He slipped the battery out of his phone — these he kept — and broke the unit in half, then dropped the carcass into a bag for disposal. From a drawer he withdrew another phone and, with a sharp, bone-handled knife, his father's, he began to slice through the encasing plastic carefully, one centimeter at a time.

* * *

After disconnecting the call, the stocky man put his Samsung into the pocket of his olive drab combat jacket and, sipping excellent diner coffee, wondered where the name Echi came from.

Wasn't that some kind of foreign word? No. *Ecco*. Was that it? From an old language? Like Greek or Roman? *Ecco, therefore I am.* In his job Stan Coelho didn't have much connection with old-time writing or foreign languages, other than Spanish. And occasionally Russian, if he had to go up against the Brighton Beach crew in Brooklyn.

He should read more. He should learn more.

Another bite of sloppy eggs.

So, *Ecco* Rinaldo was dead and a very important delivery had gone missing.

Well, this was a mess.

Perched on a creaky stool, he was finishing breakfast at a diner on the Upper East Side, eggs over easy, toast to mop, and turkey sausage, which because it was turkey was supposed to have less calories and fat than the other kind, the real kind. Probably didn't, though. Turkey fat, pig fat, both pretty much the same.

He felt his girth press against his belt, as if the meal was already expanding his forty-four-inch waist. It wasn't, Coelho was sure, but the imagined bloating felt real. He'd get the weight under control soon.

"Hey, honey, refill." He tapped the coffee cup. "And that Danish. The cheese one. And the bill."

"Sure thing."

He reached for his wallet but he reached carefully. He was carrying a Glock inside that taut waistband, pretty concealed but not absolutely concealed, and the diner was crowded. Not the place for somebody to scream, "That asshole's got a gun!"

Reflecting on the phone call a moment ago: his mission was to find the delivery, maybe find who did Rinaldo, but at this point doing that was optional. The delivery was all that mattered.

He left a bit of sausage, in caloric compensation, and chewed down half the Danish, which tasted mostly of sugar. Not that that was a negative. He poured back two slugs of coffee and ate the rest of the pastry. He wiped his mouth and his impressive moustache, as salt-and-pepper as his thick hair. Digging for bills, he left a ten and five under the plate, a generous tip. Then replaced the wallet — replacing carefully — and left the diner, walking out onto Third Avenue, congested with people headed to work, mostly going south, to Midtown. He lived in Queens, where the commute was different, mostly you took buses or walked to the subway or elevateds. It was still crowded, but not like this.

Manhattan.

Good diners here. Not much of anything else for him.

Coelho stood close to the diner and lit a cigarette. A woman passing by, dragging her overbundled kid to an overpriced school, glared at him. His return glare said, Fuck you, it's still America. He wanted to exhale smoke her way but she was gone fast, plodding along in her massive and ugly boots.

Smoking, thinking about where the delivery might be. The huge number of people streaming past seemed to flaunt the hopelessness of the mission.

At last, his phone hummed and he looked at caller ID.

"Yo."

"Still no word who bodied Rinaldo."

"Don't care about that," Coelho said. "Gimme something about the delivery. S'all we care about at this point."

The caller was some punk who ran numbers and did drop-offs and pickups for the crews. Similar to the dead Rinaldo's job. Coelho had never met him, but he was vouched for. He had an accent that seemed to be a mix of three different languages.

"The delivery arrived in town at eleven in the a.m. yesterday. Off a train from Chicago."

"I know all this. Keep going."

"Some driver picked it up in Jersey, the depot at Newark. Took it to some location in Midtown. Met Rinaldo for the transfer. Then... nobody knows what happened."

"'Some location' is not particularly fucking helpful."

"I'm working on that, man. It was the West Side, near the water, someplace they wouldn't be seen."

Wouldn't be seen? Midtown west wasn't Midtown central but it was still one of the busiest places on the face of the earth. Hell, the traffic to and from the highway running along the Hudson alone meant ten thousand witnesses an hour.

But, he reflected, Rinaldo may have been stupid enough to get himself killed but he wasn't stupid when it came to his job, especially a task entrusted to him by the infamous Miguel Ángel.

"K," Coelho told his contact. "I'll head over there now. But stay on top of it. I need an address. There'll be something in it for you. Promise."

"Thanks."

They disconnected.

Zipping his jacket up, not so much for the cold, which it really wasn't, but just so his concealed gun stayed concealed, Coelho started the walk to Midtown, calculating how many calories the hike would burn.

A fair amount, he reflected happily and bought a hotdog and a Coke to tide him over on the journey.

* * *

"There's more here than it seemed last night," said Mel Cooper dubiously, nodding at the mass of evidence from the Echi Rinaldo crime scene, laid out on the evidence tables in Rhyme's town house.

"Is there really?" Rhyme glanced over at the slightly built, bespectacled man. The response had been ironic. The meaning: What's the point of stating the obvious? Beneath was the subtextual message: If there's so much perhaps we should be analyzing and not discussing.

Cooper was the preeminent forensic lab technician in the NYPD's crime scene operation, headquartered in Queens. He frequently worked with Rhyme and Sachs, manning the equipment here. He'd arrived last night, worked until 4 a.m., headed home to his mother's house for a bit of sleep and was now back, robed and masked like a surgeon.

"We're not making any progress."

"Now, *that* is a valid observation."

The analyses of the effluvia from the streets of Midtown was yielding no leads, and so Rhyme considered next steps. He said to Cooper, "Rinaldo's burner phone's still with Szarnek down at computer crimes. It had some kind of wipe feature, but they're trying to restore the data." Rhyme wheeled to a table, on which a Post-it note had been pasted. It read: *Found within six feet of victim.* It was a mountain and included two dozen different shoe print and fifty different fingerprint samples. Three used condoms. Rhyme grimaced, not at the distasteful aspect of these particular items but because while the odds were minimal that the killer took time before or after the slaughter to have protected sex, he might actually have done so.

And, though Rhyme despised clichés, the adage about no stone being left unturned was the bylaw for crime scene work.

There were also piles of trash — literally — from the route where the blood trail began to the place near the middle of the alley where Rinaldo had died.

Rhyme made a decision. "Let's focus on where he'd been earlier and who he'd been in contact with. He was a deliveryman... if we can pin him to locations where he made his deliveries, we might find somebody he hooked up with."

"And who had a motive to kill him."

"Maybe. That'll be for Amelia to find out. Our job is just to find the where and the who."

As he surveyed the evidence that might be helpful in their new task, Cooper asked, "Any chance Lon'll be up for working the case? I was talking to him last week. He seemed a bit better."

Rhyme shook his head. Lon Sellitto, his former partner and the Major Cases detective who officially ran the investigations Rhyme assisted on as a consultant, was still ill, laid low by a poison attack in a recent case. "I asked, and he's still out of commission."

Cooper sighed. "Even after all these months?"

He'd nearly died. It was a medical miracle that he'd been saved.

Rhyme dismissed the subject with: "Let's get to it. Anything on the body or on the bed of the truck or tire treads that'll give us a history of where he was earlier in the day?"

It was clear there'd been a struggle and Rinaldo had fought his assailant. Locard's Principle, named for the French criminalist Edmond Locard, holds that there is always a transfer of evidence between perp and crime scene or perp and victim. This is especially true in the case of physical struggle. Ideally, Rinaldo would have dug some telltale DNA from his killer's skin with his fingernail as he fought the man. Now, reading the ME's and Sachs's reports, they learned that Rinaldo had worn gloves. Trace from the gloves and his coat, run through the gas chromatograph/mass spectrometer, revealed no chemicals that might lead them to a particular location or suggest a profession that the killer might have had or hairs or other DNA-rich evidence.

Rhyme sighed. "Tires and Rinaldo's shoes. Let's see what they collected."

Fortunately the truck had fairly new tires — and the victim had worn treaded running shoes — so there was a fair amount of soil trace in both.

Cooper prepared a sample for the GC/MS. As he did so, Rhyme squinted and turned away from the machine. He'd heard the faint sound of a key in the front door (after the accident rendered him disabled, he was convinced that his surviving senses grew more acute). Thom was in the kitchen, so this would be Sachs, who'd left earlier to pick up Rinaldo's son at a Child and Family Services facility and take him to an emergency foster care family. He was glad she'd returned; he wanted her insights into the case.

But then he heard something in addition to her footfalls, something that troubled him.

Another set of steps, softer.

He sighed.

"What's wrong?" Mel Cooper asked, noting the expression.

He didn't answer.

Sachs turned the corner with a companion. The boy, strapping and dark-skinned, with crewcut black hair, stopped in the parlor doorway, eyes wide as he gazed at the equipment.

Sachs gave a faint smile at, Rhyme supposed, what would be his look of dismay. She said, "This is Javier."

"Hi," Mel Cooper said.

Rhyme nodded, forcing a smile onto his face.

The boy nodded cautiously then turned back to the machinery.

Sachs paused only a moment and, knowing what Rhyme would be thinking, said, "Javier's not staying here. The foster family's not far away, on the West Side. I told him I'd stop here and he could meet the people who are going to catch the man who killed his father."

The boy fiddled with what looked like a pencil box. It had a picture of some boxy cartoon characters and the word "Minecraft" on it. He also held a tablet of drawing paper and Rhyme could see some sketches of similar characters. They were pretty good for a child of his age.

"Well, yes." Rhyme nodded at him. What was the boy's name again? He'd forgotten already. "We're doing—"

"You in one of those chairs. Damn. Wheels. And a motor. I've seen them. Why?"

"I can't walk."

He blinked. "You can't walk? How d'you play soccer?"

"I can't."

"Shit."

Rhyme now smiled genuinely. "Yeah. Shit."

Sachs said, "Javier? These men're going to use all this equipment, like you see on TV. They're going to find that man."

"Yeah." The boy's eyes had grown cloudy again. He wasn't going to cry, Rhyme assessed, and he wasn't going to give in to a temper tantrum. But he seemed to be shrinking, withdrawing.

"I'll be back in a half hour, Rhyme," Sachs said.

She turned. Javier, however, remained where he was, staring at Rhyme's chair. He pointed to a screen — the one attached to the gas chromatograph/mass spectrometer. He said, "There's this game. FIFA. A video game. You know FIFA?"

He had no idea. He said, "Sure."

"This game, you can play soccer. Any team you want. Chelsea. Liverpool. Galaxy. It's cool. You can play it in your chair. You don't have to run around. You can play it sitting there."

"Thanks, Javier."

"Yeah. It's a good game."

Then he turned and together he and Sachs walked out the door.

"Seems like a good kid," Cooper said. "Too bad what happened."

"The trace, Mel," Rhyme reminded. "The trace." And nodded emphatically at the GC/MS.

* * *

The foster family, living in a small townhouse on the Upper West Side, seemed perfect for their task. Unflappable, calm, casual. Just the sort to take the edge off children wrested from traumatic home lives.

Sally Abbott was a pretty brunette — in her thirties, Amelia Sachs estimated. She was in jeans and a burgundy sweater. Her husband, a few years older, short but athletic, wore an affable smile and shook Sachs's hand vigorously, then turned his attention to Javier. He engaged the boy immediately in conversation — all of it about the boy himself, what he liked to do and eat and, of course, what teams he liked. They appeared easygoing but the Child and Family Services caseworker had assured Sachs that some of their past placements had been kids from similar backgrounds as Javier — even tougher ones. However the boy reacted to them, the couple would be prepared to deal.

The attention and good cheer behind these first few minutes seemed natural but Sachs also guessed this was standard procedure for the foster process. There would be times in the future for serious talk, tears at night, angry outbursts at fate or at spilled soda or at nothing at all, but people like this generous couple knew their job. Now was simply the time for welcome and reassurance.

Peter Abbott took the boy to show him to his room. Javier wheeled the suitcase himself — he wouldn't let the man take it.

Sachs was glad for the moment alone with Mrs. Abbott. She said in a low voice, "There's no reason to be concerned, but I'm having an officer stay outside in an unmarked car. You'll see it, an SUV." She explained that they were still investigating his father's killing. Her belief was that it was probably a random murder. The incident did not appear to be an organized crime hit; the circumstances suggested a chance mugging gone bad or a personal fight. "Still, until we know more, we just want to be safe."

The foster mother said she understood and that this had happened before, usually in the context of protecting children from natural parents who were unstable and under restraining orders. But she asked, "Can we go to the park, to games?"

"Oh, sure. Officer Lamont'll just hang out with you. He'll be in plain clothes. Javier met him. They get along well. They're Mets fans."

She smiled. "So'm I. Peter roots for the Cubs... I know, I know. But I love him anyway."

Sachs too offered a grin.

She and Mrs. Abbott then walked to the boy's bedroom, on the second floor, and Sachs was impressed. It was clean and cozy, filled with gender-neutral toys and decorations. A desktop computer with a sign: *Call Mom Sally or Dad Peter before you go online.*

She approved of that.

Sachs didn't know the protocol about physical contact but when she said goodbye to the boy, he threw his arms around her. "You come see me, Miss Amelia?"

"Sure will!" Sachs hugged back firmly. She handed both him and Mrs. Abbott business cards. "Anything, anytime, you need me, please, give me a call."

She watched Javier drop down on the bed, unzip his Minecraft box and take from it some colored pencils. He began to draw.

Outside, Sachs had taken no more than two steps toward her Ford Torino when her phone hummed. It was Rhyme.

"Hi, I just dropped him off. He seems pretty—"

His voice cut her off. "We've got a lead. You know the old armory on West Fifty?"

"Sure." It was a decrepit abandoned facility dating from early in the last century. The place was, she'd read, scheduled for demolition... though it seemed that articles about that fate had been popping up in the papers for decades.

"How'd you nail it?"

"Rinaldo's shoes and his truck's tread marks. Mel and I found trace from horse shit and recycled oil. The front of the armory's on Five-one and Eleven but — Mel checked — there's a back entrance at Fifty and Ten, near a stable where they house Central Park horses. And next to that is a recycled oil warehouse."

"I'm on my way."

* * *

Stan Coelho was smoking, leaning against an office building wall, on the far West Side of Manhattan, admiring the *Intrepid* aircraft carrier. Big effing ship. He'd never been in an armed service, but if he had been, he'd want to be a sailor on a boat like that.

Well, now that he studied it, a *new* carrier. This one looked like the accommodations wouldn't be exactly four star.

A pointless glance at his phone. He put it away.

Just as impatience got the better of him and he pushed off his perch to find a greasy spoon to duck into for lunch, the Samsung hummed. The sound announced an arriving text.

'Bout time.

Ah, great! The punk had come through. Bless him. The text reported the location where Ecco, well, *Echi*, Rinaldo had picked up the delivery yesterday at eleven thirty in the morning. No more details about where he might've taken it for safekeeping. But the transfer point was a good start. He texted back, acknowledging the info.

The location was only about three blocks away. Coelho turned in the direction and made his way over the sidewalks, which here ran in front of car dealerships and repair shops, graphic design studios, small ad agencies, warehouses, apartments and what he'd been checking out earlier — the oiliest of greasy spoons. It was changing, though, and maybe someday soon the 'hood would be the new chic, now that most of the rest of Manhattan — even Harlem — was getting too cool, too hipster for words.

In ten minutes he spotted the building that he sought.

The West Side Armory was quite a piece of work. Two stories high, resembling a redbrick castle. Downright ugly, Coelho thought, though who was he to talk? He'd never bothered to pitch out the pink flamingos that had been standing one-legged in front of his Queens bungalow when he'd moved in two years ago. (And the color of his brick — dried blood red — was the same as the armory's.)

Looking about, making sure no one was paying him any mind, he walked to the entrance of the place on Eleventh Avenue. The graffiti-marred doors were locked and chained. They were ten feet tall and solid oak — the place was, after all, an *armory*, and presumably had once contained weapons of mass destruction (for the time), which the National Guard or army wished to keep out of the hands of assorted bad guys.

No entrance this way.

He circled around the building and finally noticed, on 50th Street, a small door whose lock just didn't look right. He eased up to it and, again making certain that no one was watching, tested the knob. Yes, the lock and deadbolt had been jimmied — some time ago, to judge from the rust — and with effort he muscled the panel open. He was greeted with a smell of mold and mildew and urine that nearly took his breath away. He forced down the cough, and nausea, and slipped inside.

The door let into a storeroom of some kind, now empty, except for evidence that revealed why the door was still in use: needles and crack pipes and tubes that had once held rock. The den was empty now, thank God, so Coelho did not have to crack heads with his Glock.

He eased into a hallway and then made his way to what seemed to be an archway. The place was huge — the corridor disappeared a block away into darkness. No, Rinaldo wasn't stupid at all. This was the perfect place to make the transfer. Coelho wondered: Did he hide it *here*? Were there basements? Hidden rooms? It might take days to search and find it.

And if he'd merely taken delivery here in the armory what clues could he or anyone possibly find that might suggest where the shipment was now?

Hopeless. Well, here he was. So he'd have to—

A noise.

Freezing, Coelho realized he wasn't alone.

It had been a tap or snap, coming from inside but some distance far away — on the other side of the archway, which opened presumably to the main arena of the armory. Drawing his pistol, he started forward, keeping close to the walls and watching carefully where he placed his feet to avoid both tripping and giving away his presence.

Heart pounding, the two hotdogs churning in his gut, he swapped his gun to his left hand, wiped his right palm on his slacks and then took the gun again in his other grip. Closer to the archway, he paused. Then: a quick look out. At the far end of the open area — it really was huge — he saw a figure, fifty yards away, standing with arms crossed. The man was looking around. Because a doorway was open behind him, the back light made it impossible to see any details.

But then the person stepped slightly to the side, and he decided this was probably a woman. Something about the stance, the size of the hips. Though her hair was up, or under some kind of cap.

Apparently satisfied with whatever she'd been doing, she picked up a large suitcase, it seemed, and turned, walking to the doorway.

Was this a coincidence? Was she a building inspector or real estate developer? Or was this about Rinaldo? And the delivery? And, if so, had she found something important?

Keeping the gun in his hand, finger near but not on the trigger, Coelho jogged as fast as he dared to the open doorway she'd just vanished through.

But just as he got close, the first side of the double door, then the second, slammed shut. And he heard it lock.

Goddamn it. He tried to push it open but the panels were sealed fast.

He sprinted back, his bulk ramping up his heart rate and breathing. Don't let me die here, he thought. Christ, it might take months to find my body.

And don't let me puke.

But, no coronaries, or regurgitation, today. He made it back to the jimmied door through which he'd entered and eased out, pushing it shut again. Once on the sidewalk, his gun still in hand but hidden under his jacket, he continued along the sidewalk fast, circling the building. As he turned the corner, he slowed and caught his breath.

The intruder was standing at the curbside, beside the large suitcase he'd seen. She was a tall redheaded woman. She looked around, with suspicious eyes, and he ducked behind one of the armory's abutments, but she wasn't gazing in his direction. She was focusing on the street near her. Her posture suggested that she was armed; as she studied the area her right hand was near her hip, fingers curled slightly, as if ready to draw. Coelho knew this because it was the pose he often adopted if a gunfight loomed.

Who the hell is she? Working for a rival gang? Working for the shipper? A cop?

He'd have to find out.

Get close, as soon as she got into her car he'd leap into the passenger seat and press a gun against her side. Then make sure she didn't buckle up, though he would. And he'd force her to drive to some deserted spot. Then get answers.

Hand gripping his pistol, still hidden, he crossed the street and moved east, in her direction, using parked cars and trucks for cover. Ahead, at the intersection, was a large McDonald's, under a big billboard advertising the place — a sign of the gentrification he'd been thinking of earlier.

The hour was lunchtime and the sidewalk here was crowded. He was lost in the throngs of people entering and leaving the restaurant.

As he approached he saw she was quite pretty. What the hell was she up to? Some hot babe in a muscle car, poking around the place where a half million dollars of very illegal shit had been transferred. She could be a skirt working for a gangbanger, who'd picked her to minimize suspicion, in his search for the mysterious delivery.

Hell, that was a sexist thought. The bitch might be an OG *herself*, some rival to Morales. The world was changing. It was only a matter of time until a woman rose up high in the organized crime scene of New York and was crowned an Original Gangster.

Gangsterette? Coelho allowed himself the humorous thought.

She set the suitcase into the trunk, slammed it and pulled out her phone to make a call.

As soon as she finished and got into the front seat, he'd make his move.

He now broke through the crowd and started across the street toward the Torino.

But she moved fast. Yanking open the door and tossing the phone onto the passenger seat. In seconds, the car fired up and she was skidding — actually laying a patch of rubber as she sped away.

Shit.

Well, at least he'd had some confirmation that the arsenal had a connection with Rinaldo and the infamous delivery. Why else would an armed woman, who drove like that, be interested?

A connection... What the hell was it?

He glanced at a Greek diner behind him, smelling the garlic and grilling fish.

Then he thought about his boss and told himself: No, get to work.

* * *

"What's this discovery you're so excited about?" Mel Cooper asked Amelia Sachs as she walked quickly into Rhyme's parlor.

"Gloves."

"Really?" Cooper asked, enthusiastic.

"I'll give you the whole story," she said. "In addition to the oil operation and the stable — that told you Rinaldo'd been to the armory — there're two restaurants across from the back entrance to the place. A McDonalds and a Greek diner. I found two witnesses who're pretty sure that—"

"Pretty sure—"

"Rhyme," she warned.

He shrugged. "Pray continue."

"Who're pretty sure that two white trucks drove through back entrance about eleven thirty yesterday morning."

"How'd they get in?"

"Locks were picked, I'm pretty sure. Scratch marks. The doors closed and nobody saw what happened then or when they left. The state owns the place and I called their real estate division and they had the maintenance service let me in. Creepy place. If you're ever inclined to make a horror film, that's the set for it. The place basically has a dirt floor, so I took soil samples. I found treads that even without comparison I recognized as Rinaldo's. The other truck there? The treads were pretty bad. It'll be impossible to get any ID'ing tread marks from them."

"You were mentioning gloves." Rhyme was growing impatient.

She held up a plastic bag. "Latex."

"Ah, that *is* good news." Latex gloves, unlike cloth, pick up fingerprints quite well (on the inside) and have adhesive properties that retain trace. Smart criminals burn them into nothing, the not-so-smart throw them out, for police to find and, soon thereafter, make all sort of helpful discoveries to aid in arrest and conviction.

"Friction ridges first."

Wearing his own set of gloves — a similar shade of blue — Mel Cooper extracted and tested them. There were two, a right and a left. Rhyme hoped they belonged to whomever Rinaldo had met in the armory, as they already had Rinaldo's identity.

They did not, as it turned out. Only the victim's prints were inside the gloves.

Rhyme was frowning. "Curious. He left them in the armory after the meeting. He wasn't that concerned that they'd be found so he wasn't particularly troubled about leaving his prints there."

"But," Sachs continued his thought, "he *was* worried about prints on whatever he was holding — something that either he or the other driver had with them."

"He was a deliveryman," Rhyme pointed out. "And since the truck was empty when he was killed, and locked, he either transferred something to the other driver or took delivery and then dropped it off at another location." He frowned. "What the hell was the shipment?... Mel," Rhyme ordered, "find out what trace there is on the outside of the gloves."

He prepared the sample.

As he did, Rhyme's computer dinged with the sound of an incoming email. He read the subject and the sender. "Ah, it's from Rodney."

Rodney Szarnek, their computer crimes expert down in One Police Plaza.

"He cracked Rinaldo's phone," Rhyme said, reading. "It was a burner, naturally."

Prepaid mobiles with no link to the purchaser or his or her actual address had made cops' lives far more difficult.

Rhyme continued. "It had only four texts. And five incoming calls from the same number — also an untraceable burner, now out of service. The calls weren't answered. Voice mail wasn't set up."

She walked around behind him and he could feel her gloved hand on his shoulder, just north of the DMZ where all sensation stopped.

They read the messages. The first one, from Rinaldo's burner, was sent at eleven forty.

> Have package. Will hide. Have good place. Will meet U @ 7, where planned, with details. Tonight, you'll be the king of the dead.

And the below was the simple response

K

At four thirty there, Rinaldo had texted the other phone:

All hidden. We're good. No tails. Seems safe.

The answer again:

K

The incoming calls, Rhyme observed, were all made a few minutes apart and they started at 7:05 p.m., presumably his client calling with increasing agitation to inquire as to why Rinaldo was not at the delivery site. He had been murdered, Rhyme recalled, at 6 p.m.

Sachs said, "So, that answers the question. Rinaldo took delivery at the armory and then hid it somewhere, in anticipation of taking it to the final consignee that night."

King of the dead, Rhyme reflected. He had a thought. "Mel, do you have the results of the trace on the gloves?"

"I do." The tech said, "Present are—"

Rhyme said, "Lead, antimony, and barium, calcium, silicon… and, I'll go out on a limb, rubber."

"Well, no silicon, but yes, everything else. And in significant amounts. How on earth did you figure that out?" He was smiling.

But the expression faded as he regarded Rhyme's grim face. "King of the dead," he mused. "The chemicals're gunshot residue. And the rubber from a silencer of some sort. I said 'out on a limb.'" He scowled. "But of course there *had* to be rubber. From baffles of a silencer. Rinaldo tested the product he was picking up to make sure it worked… and he could hardly fire off a gun in Midtown without using a silencer."

Sachs said, "And given the amounts of the residue you mentioned, it's automatic weapons?"

"I hadn't thought of that. But yes, of course. There's our answer: Mr. Echi Rinaldo was taking delivery of machine guns. And I'd imagine quite a few of them, given the size of the trucks involved. The good news, I suppose, is that he didn't deliver them to the purchaser."

The bad, which went unstated, was that a large number of deadly weapons were loose in the City of New York, free for the taking to whoever found them first.

The mantle of King of the Dead was apparently up for grabs.

* * *

As head of the 128 Lords, Miguel Ángel Morales was largely oblivious to politics.

Oh, there were Harlem councilmen and the occasional cop who had to be paid off (the NYPD was a lot less receptive to bribes than it used to be, though). But at levels higher than city hall and various administrative bureaus, politics didn't much come into play for an OG like Morales.

He had, however, made a study of one political matter: NAFTA, the free trade agreement between Mexico, Canada and the United States, which eased trade restrictions — and the physical movement — of products over the borders.

Everyone knew it was politically correct to decry the flow of drugs moving north and the ebb of guns going in the opposite direction, and politicos and administrators made certain that loosened border controls, thanks to NAFTA, didn't facilitate this terrible commerce.

Who could argue? Morales certainly didn't.

But listening to an NPR segment about the trade agreement a year ago, an idea had occurred to him. After some research he learned that while drugs were still interdicted enthusiastically going north and guns going south, the customs system under NAFTA had grown careless when it came to these commodities going in the opposite directions. Resources, after all, were limited.

Could one, Morales asked, make money smuggling guns *north*?

On one of several trips to Mexico that he and Connie made, he learned that it was very hard to get good weapons of American or European make over the border. Fifteen thousand pesos for *Cuernos de Chivo*, "goat horns," as AK-47s were known in Mexico, and six thousand pesos for a Glock. Even realistic toy guns — used in the many of the one hundred armed (or *seemingly* armed) robberies in Mexico City alone every day — were expensive. Oh, you could negotiate some when you went to buy weapons in the pungent, filthy Tepito district of Mexico City — the drug and weapon bazaar — if you survived the experience (which a lot of people did not).

To fill this gap and bring prices down, an innovative cartel boss in Chihuahua had come up with an idea. He bought high-end guns — H&Ks, Glocks, Rugers — and he had them reverse engineered, created the tools and dies necessary for their manufacture and went into business, manufacturing quality firearms under the guise of creating auto parts. There were so many American manufacturers shifting jobs to Mexico that nobody noticed that his operation did not, in fact, have a connection with Ford or GM or Toyota.

The cartel head's main market was Mexico and points south. Morales, though, saw an opportunity and decided to go into partnership with Señor Guadalupe. He commissioned an order and paid for it, then arranged for transport north. The NAFTA-sanctioned trucks, the partners reasoned, would proceed largely unimpeded into the United States and, if they were stopped, it was to check for drugs; those Labradors and Malinois were certainly clever but also scent-blind when it came to stocks and receivers of deadly weapons. They smelled after all just like car parts.

The shipment that Echi Rinaldo had picked up in the armory yesterday was Morales's first purchase and its disappearance was a real problem. He had buyers lined up, true, but more troubling: his reputation. He wanted to be, as he'd said in all seriousness to Rinaldo and his compadres, New York's King of the Dead, and anything that diminished that reputation was not acceptable. He certainly had the product: These weapons were among the most sophisticated in the world, some with laser and radar sights, some so silent they were — as Guadalupe had told him — no louder than a hiccup *de un bebé*.

Bullets too. Special ones, engineered by the cartel man's best gunsmiths.

But having such fine merchandise made this failing, this glitch, all the more embarrassing.

He debated once more the question of whether or not he should have trusted Rinaldo with this assignment. Well, that wasn't quite the right inquiry. Echi Rinaldo had done many jobs for him and trust was not an issue. Where he questioned his judgment was the caution with which he'd approached the delivery. Morales had delegated to Rinaldo the job of collecting the half million dollars' worth of machine guns solely in case the feds or someone else had tipped to the shipment. Rinaldo had been told of the risk and had willingly taken it on — for a substantial fee. They agreed he wouldn't transfer the goods immediately, either. He would drive around all day and make his regular deliveries and, if no one appeared to be following or if he sensed no other threat, then he would meet Morales and tell him where the guns were stashed.

At the time, these precautions made sense.

But now they had, perhaps, been his undoing.

Miguel Ángel Morales was presently strolling through Central Park, making his way to a park bench where he regularly met his people. It was near the Sheep Meadow and therefore easy to spot anyone conducting surveillance.

He'd received a text from his lieutenant that the man had made some discoveries and wanted to relay them as soon as possible.

The gang overlord continued down the meandering path to the bench. He sat and scanned the area for any signs that he was being watched.

No, it was clear. Years of living a gang boss's life had given him acute senses, and he trusted these.

A glance at his watch.

Fifteen minutes until his lieutenant appeared, with, Morales prayed, good news.

* * *

Amelia Sachs was back in the armory, once again dressed in her crime scene coveralls.

And, as again, glad for the face mask. This was meant to prevent her DNA from tainting the evidence she might collect but it also had the added benefit of filtering out the overwhelming scent of mildew and mold and pee... and, of course, protecting her from the accompanying spores, which would do no one's lungs any good.

She paused and listened occasionally — the sounds of traffic. Other sounds too. Creaks and groans.

If you're ever inclined to make a horror film, that's the set for it...

What she was finding was helpful forensically but also troubling. Yes, it seemed that Echi Rinaldo had tried out an automatic weapon here. She was digging slugs out of the dirt about thirty yards from where his delivery truck had parked here. She might find fingerprints on them, which would lead to the seller of the ammunition — a perp in his own right, even if he had nothing to do with Rinaldo's death.

And the troubling part? With a grimace, she gazed at the bullets she'd bagged. They were "cop killers"—and of a style she'd never seen. They could pierce body armor but, once through the Kevlar, would expand inside the victim's flesh. A single shot, even to nonvital organs, would probably be fatal, thanks to massive hemorrhaging.

She collected more bullets, then, judging trajectory, looked for but did not find any shell casings. Rinaldo or the other truck driver would have taken those with them. She assembled the evidence and crouched to put the Baggies into a milk carton.

It was then that she heard a sound from the archway that led into the corridor circumnavigating the armory. And not a *Friday the 13th* soundtrack sound. A footfall. Somebody was there, moving closer, through the shadows.

Rising fast, she reached for her weapon.

Then from behind, a man's voice. "Don't bother."

She froze and turned to see a heavyset man, with salt and pepper hair and a large moustache of the same shades. He was holding a gun pointed roughly in her direction. It was a small Glock, the .380. She judged angles. Her own pistol, a larger one, 9mm, was strapped outside her overalls —

yes, there was a risk of contamination but she would never be zippered away from her weapon.

But no, she judged, she couldn't draw in time to stop him from shooting. If he went for a chest shot, though, the vest beneath the overalls would give her time to drop and draw.

A double tap in her head — tactically wise but a harder shot — that would be the end.

But as it turned out there was no gunplay.

The man looked at the NYPD Crime Scene Unit logo on the overalls and slipped his weapon away. "I was saying: Don't bother with him." Nodding toward the archway where the sound had come from. "He's just some meth-head. Harmless."

Then he reached into his pocket and withdrew a shield case. He displayed the badge and the ID.

"Stan Coelho. ATF." He gave a laugh. "Well, now *ATFE*, since they gave us explosives too. When I first saw you, I thought you might be working for some crews. But now—" He gestured toward her outfit. "—looks like one of the good guys. Well, gals." He frowned. "Or shouldn't I be using that word nowadays?"

* * *

Miguel Ángel Morales saw his lieutenant striding briskly along the walk toward the bench.

Raphael Ortiz sat down on the bench, though three feet away.

"No," Morales said, "It's clear. I've been watching."

The skinny man, thirty to fifty, impossible to tell, moved closer. He pulled his gaudy yellow and brown checkered jacket closer. Morales paid the lieutenant good money. Why he dressed like this was always a mystery.

"We know Rinaldo took delivery of the guns at the armory eleven thirty or so. And we know as of four he'd hidden the delivery somewhere. And everything looked good."

They knew this from the texts, yes.

Ortiz continued, "In between he made a half dozen deliveries around Manhattan — all of them legit. A washer/dryer, some tomato sauce to a couple of restaurants. Auto parts."

That was part of the plan, staying legal. Morales didn't want him to get busted for some little drug drop off and the delivery of guns would get spotted in the process.

"Now I've reconstructed his route for most of the day. But there's no sign that he dropped off our delivery anywhere he went on his legit route. But — here's the thing — he was unaccounted for, for an hour between his last two deliveries. And it wouldn't take that long to drive from one to the other."

Morales's spirits were buoyed. If Ortiz and his people had been unable to track Rinaldo for the entire day, that would have been a problem. But just an hour or so of a gap? The man's diversion to the hiding place could probably be reconstructed.

"All right. Let's proceed. Like I was saying before."

Ortiz nodded. "I'll need a little time to make some arrangements."

It was harder and harder nowadays to get rid of bodies. You had to be absolutely certain that they disappeared completely. And it wasn't just dogs. They had special radar that could find a body twenty feet underground.

"You'll be ready by five?"

Ortiz considered. A nod.

Morales gave his man an address verbally and asked him to repeat it. Which he did. The mousy man had a great memory.

"Good."

And both men rose. Without a word of farewell they turned in different directions and walked away.

* * *

"We're not the only ones working the case."

Sachs was explaining to Rhyme and Cooper that an Alcohol, Tobacco and Firearms agent, Stan Coelho, had been following the shipment of automatic weapons from the other end, the shipper. "They got a tip from some snitch in Chicago, and were following it east from a warehouse on the south side."

"Supply side investigating, you could say." Rhyme was pleased with the joke.

Sachs continued, "Came into the area by train. New Jersey. Coelho got a tip that it was being transferred at the armory but that was today. Rinaldo was long gone. They don't have any other leads."

"What was the source?"

"He said they think it came from Mexico or Canada, but intel there hasn't been helpful."

"This agent. Is he—"

"Legit. Yes." Sachs was at that moment online with the secure database, reading. Coelho was in good standing. She looked over at Rhyme. "His boss, the regional agent in charge, gave him the orders to find the shipment. Or heads will roll." She laughed. "This Coelho, he's quite a piece of work. Right out of the movies. He said his boss has a hard-on the size of Maine to find the shipment. Coelho said, 'Why Maine? I would've picked Texas.' He seemed genuinely perplexed."

"Any thoughts on who killed Rinaldo?"

"No. All ATF cares about is the shipment."

It was true, Rhyme reflected, that the victim in the murder case, normally the hub of an investigation, was presently almost an afterthought.

"So they don't have anything more than we do?"

"No. He's been in touch with Homeland Security, FBI, CIA. There's no terrorist connection that anybody knows about. ATF thinks it's a for-profit thing. He said the BK gangs might be looking for firepower like this."

Rhyme sighed. "Cop-killing rounds, big ones, two-twenty-threes. Fully silenced. Just what we need on the street."

"I kept the rounds I dug up, but Coelho took some pictures. He's going to check their database and see what he can find."

Mel Cooper approached. "Hope they have better luck than I do. They're homemade. No known brand. Though built to high tolerances. Professional. Oh, and no prints. Whoever loaded them into the mag wore gloves."

Rhyme leaned his head back against the chair's rest. "And the evidence doesn't show any indication of where Rinaldo went after the transfer at the armory. Somehow we'll have to reconstruct his whereabouts during the day."

"You're forgetting," she said.

He looked at the evidence.

"Not that," she chided. "Rinaldo wasn't alone, remember. At least for a portion of the day."

"Oh, the boy."

"Javier."

"Javier." Rhyme grimaced. "An eight-year-old, though? Who's undoubtedly traumatized? What would he know?"

"At least he won't have a motive to lie."

He conceded that. "Well, ask him."

Sachs called the foster couple. Sally Abbott answered the phone.

"It's Amelia Sachs. The detective that brought Javier over to you."

"Sure. Yes. How are you?"

"Fine. You're on speaker with my partner here. How's Javier doing?"

Rhyme lifted his eyebrow, impatiently. Sachs ignored him.

"Quiet. Doesn't want to talk. But adjusting pretty well, all things considered." She was speaking softly and Sachs guessed that Javier wasn't far away. "He's drawing up a storm with those colored pencils of his and he and Peter watched some soccer."

Rhyme cleared his throat.

"Do you have some idea who killed his father?" A very soft whisper.

"No, but it would be helpful if he could tell us a few things."

"Sure." There was a rustling of the phone and Rhyme heard the woman call, "Javier, I've got Miss Amelia on the phone. She wants to ask you a few questions." She too hit the speaker button, Rhyme could hear.

"Hi. How're you?"

"Good, Javier. How you doing?"

"Okay."

"I'd like to know a few things."

"Sure, I guess."

"When did you meet your dad yesterday?"

"I don't know. He came by the school and picked me up. Maybe eleven or twelve. He said I didn't have to go to school in the afternoon."

Sachs continued, "Did you go with him to armory on the West Side? Right after school."

"I don't know. What's that?"

"An old building near the river."

"I don't know. Building?"

The foster mother knew it. She said, "Javier, you know that big aircraft carrier on the river? That museum. Have you ever been there?"

"Yeah, I been." He added quietly, "I been with my daddy."

Sally added, "Well, where Ms. Amelia is talking about is a big building sort of near the ship. There's a McDonald's there."

Sachs said, "With your father, yesterday? Did you go there? A big red-brick building. Takes up the whole block."

"No. I never seen that."

So Rinaldo picked up the guns before he collected his son.

"Now, you drove around with him all day."

"Yeah."

"And he dropped his deliveries off. Did you help him?"

"I'm just a kid."

Sachs had to smile, and she heard Sally Abbott chuckle.

"You stayed in the truck."

"Yeah."

"Do you remember where he went to make his deliveries?"

"I don't know. Sorta."

"Tell you what: I know you like to draw, right?"

"Yeah. It's okay."

"Could you draw some pictures in your tablet where you and your father went? Maybe write down anything you remember too. I'll come by later and we can look at it together."

"I guess."

She added, "Sally? Could you help him?"

The woman agreed that they would and she'd call Sachs when the boy had some thoughts.

"Javier? You need anything?"

"No."

Sachs said goodbye and they disconnected. She looked at Rhyme with a coy smile. "You don't seem to feel that's a productive form of inquiry."

"An eight-year-old drawing pictures of his recollections in crayon? In a word, no."

"It's colored pencil," she corrected.

"Well, now, there's a difference for you. Can we get back to the evidence, please and thank you?"

* * *

Studying the windows, the dancing shadows.

Hidden in the below-ground alcove of an apartment across the tree-lined street, Raphael Ortiz gazed at the town house on the Upper West Side, the home of foster parents Peter and Sally Abbott. This was the address that Miguel Ángel Morales had recited to him not long ago as they sat on the bench in windy Central Park. The arrangements for body disposal were complete and he was pleased to see he'd arrived here a few minutes early. It was 4:50 p.m. He imagined that Miguel Ángel would be pleased too. The man appreciated punctuality.

The shades of the town house were up, but lacy curtains, wafting in the breeze, obscured the view inside. Occasionally, he noted, there came a flicker of light, blue and gray and white, and he knew the television was on. He wondered if Rinaldo's boy was watching the set, and what; was the kid interested in cartoons?

When Ortiz was Javier's age he hadn't watched much TV. The family had one — everybody in the Bronx neighborhood did — but cable was crappy and it went out frequently. Probably stolen by his old man. He envied the boys and girls at school who'd talk about episodes of *Law and Order* and *Walker, Texas Ranger*. The girls loved *Blossom* and *Full House*.

A car cruised past. Several more. Ortiz, though, stayed unseen. He was careful, watching the faint wisp of exhaust from the unmarked police SUV. He didn't know if the cop inside was constantly studying the doorway and the traffic on the street, or was there merely as a deterrent and he was content to listen to the radio or read.

But he would assume the cop was vigilant as a wolf.

Miguel Ángel was never emotional, never raised his voice. But he was also a viper, known to kill easily, even those he seemed fond of. Thinking of the time Santos was smoking on a job at a warehouse in Hell's Kitchen. He tossed out his cigarette carelessly and it set a small fire. That set off the alarm, which brought the fire department.

The crew lost a smooth thirty thousand from what would have been an easy payroll check cashing service heist.

Miguel Ángel had personally tied a weight to Santos's waist and pushed him into the East River, near the sewage treatment facility in Queens.

His hand close to the Smith and Wesson in his back pocket, Ortiz now slipped out of hiding and walked up the street to the intersection, turned left and into the alley behind the townhouse complex. Staying close to the back walls, he moved slowly forward, over cobblestones, the alley cleaner than most in the city. He was counting back doors. The Abbotts' was the sixth building on the left.

Ortiz had just reached the third when a shadow appeared fast from the right and behind him.

Shit...

He gasped as a massive set of fingers closed on his own hand — the one reaching instinctively toward his pistol. An arm gripped his shoulders and tugged him roughly backward and closer to the wall. He struggled to break free but the assailant was far stronger.

He smelled a whiff of some sour aftershave and a head was next to his ear, so close that he felt beard stubble against his lobe.

"Quiet," came the command, a guttural voice.

Ortiz nodded.

The pressure relaxed completely and he turned. His lids lowered briefly in relief. He'd thought, for a moment, that there'd been a second cop, one in the alleyway, who'd nailed him. But no, it wasn't a cop. Though technically he *was* a law enforcer. Stan Coelho, officially working for the ATF but making most of his money as an informant and all around badass for Miguel Ángel Morales.

"Jesus. Almost shit my pants."

Coelho whispered, "The SUV in front?"

"Yeah?" Ortiz took to whispering too.

"It's empty." The ATF agent pointed up the alley. Ortiz could make out, just barely, faint motion from the back service doorway of the Abbotts' apartment. Ah, it was the cop from the stakeout, Ortiz understood. Ah, not a bad idea. You leave an SUV running in front of the place you're guarding — and an SUV with darkened windows, hard to see inside. Then the driver slips behind the building. Anyone wanting to break in would avoid the front door and its General Motors bouncer... and then get busted by the asshole hiding in the back.

Coelho whispering: "Come on. Here."

The big man slipped into the back doorway of the apartment building they were closest to, a recessed area, on the same side of the alley as the foster parents'. He had, apparently, already snapped the lock and deadbolt here and gestured Ortiz inside. Then, with a glance toward the cop, followed, pulling the door shut.

The ATF agent said, "We gotta go up." Lifting his eyes toward the ceiling. "Onto the roof. We go over the building—"

"We have to jump?" Ortiz was not a fan of heights.

"From one building to the other?" The massive man seemed amused. "I look like I do that? No, they're all connected. We get to their place, then down. They have the whole building."

Ortiz nodded toward the Abbott's building. "And the kid's in there?"

The man didn't answer but his look said, why you think Morales called us both here if he wasn't.

"Let's get going."

In five minutes they'd made their way down the ladder and then the stairs into the Abbotts' townhouse. The top floor, where the two men stood, guns in hands, consisted of three bedrooms, all of them — Coelho checked and reported — empty.

From below were the sounds of a television and muted conversation. The agent nodded in that direction. They started down the stairs. Normally he'd be uneasy at times like this. But he felt more or less comfortable, pleased that Coelho was here. There was going to be, Miguel Ángel had suggested, some killing and, while Ortiz shied from such work, the ATF agent — you might say — lived for it.

* * *

He forced himself not to cry out in shock.

Javier Rinaldo had come back from the bathroom and as he walked out of the john, he'd seen shadows from upstairs. He ducked into a spare bedroom and leaned out. He saw two figures coming down the stairs.

Holding guns.

No, no, no!

One of them was the guy had killed his father, he bet! Coming here to kill him too. And those nice people, the Abbotts!

Javier didn't have any idea how they'd found him but here they were. One Latino and skinny. One white and big.

What was he going to do?

They were between him and his bedroom — he couldn't get to it without being seen. He glanced at the window in this room. Then outside. He couldn't jump; it was concrete below. He couldn't fight them, either. No weapon.

But he could warn the Abbotts. There was no phone in this room but there had to be one in the big bedroom up the hall, the Abbotts'. The men with the guns moved slowly down the stairs and turned away, looking toward his room, where music from his computer game played. When they were focused on it, Javier slipped out and made his way on the carpeted floor of the hallway to the bedroom. His hands and heart shook, tears dotted his eyes.

He stepped inside fast.

And stopped. Blinking in shock. He wasn't alone. Mrs. Abbott was sitting on the bed, making a phone call.

She frowned. Filled with relief, Javier locked the door and then ran to her. "There're these men!" he whispered. "They're up the hall. They mustta come in through the roof! Call the police, you know nine one one!"

Rising, Mrs. Abbott touched her lips. "Shhh," she said. *"Silencio! No se mueven."*

Crying more tears, Javier nodded and stopped speaking. He gestured to the phone. She said nothing but walked to the door.

He gasped as she unlocked it. "No! They're out there."

Only then did he register that she'd been speaking to him in Spanish. Which she hadn't done before.

Something was wrong here. Real wrong.

The door swung open and he cried out, seeing the two men look their way. They turned and walked inside, putting their guns away. And behind them was Mr. Abbott.

Only it turned out he wasn't really Mr. Abbott. The skinny Latino man in a checkered jacket said to him. "What do we do now, Mr. Morales?"

"Bring him downstairs. We've wasted too much time."

* * *

The plan was working out.

Miguel Ángel Morales himself had come up with the idea of having his lieutenant, Raphael Ortiz, conduct surveillance and infiltrate Child and Family Services and learn which foster family Echi Rinaldo's son was going to be temporarily placed with. If they'd had more time, he would have found a couple to pretend to be the Abbotts, the foster family for Javier. But the matter had moved too quickly and the only two people available for masquerade were Morales and his wife, Connie.

They'd gotten this address and hurried here. Morales himself had murdered the Abbotts and managed to clean the place of any pictures of the real couple just before that redheaded cop brought the boy here.

Morales at first intended to use the child as bait, in hopes that whoever had killed Rinaldo had possession of the shipment and would come for the child to eliminate him as a witness. But as his triggerman, Stan Coelho, had learned — and as Morales himself had guessed — it looked like Rinaldo's killing was random and had nothing to do with the guns.

But then he came up with another idea: using the boy to track down where the deliveryman might have hidden the shipment. He'd been amused when Connie had told him that the redheaded cop, Sachs, had actually suggested the kid do the same — drawing pictures of where he and his father had been.

Now, on the main floor, Connie said, "Javier, you don't have to be afraid. These men, they didn't kill your father. They were friends with him. We're all friends."

"True, kid. We were buddies, me and your dad." Coelho was smiling, though the expression looked somewhat sinister to Morales. "I want the assholes who killed him as much as you do. I find 'em, they're fucked."

Connie frowned and clicked her tongue.

The ATF agent said, "He's heard the word before, ain't you, kid?"

Javier swallowed and gazed from face to face. "He call you Mr. Morales." Confusion filled his small face.

"We're just pretending to be the Abbotts. We're borrowing their house here."

"Where are they?" He looked around the rooms.

In the basement in garbage bags, soon to be in the Jersey swamplands, according to the plans Ortiz had made.

"They're away for a while. They agreed to help us. We have to be careful. Because the men who killed your father are very dangerous. We have to stay undercover. You know undercover, right?"

"Men who killed him?" Javier shook his head. "I only saw one man. That's all."

"But we think he was working for others." Morales was adlibbing but he thought he sounded pretty reasonable, and even a little scared, and the boy seemed to buy it. He nodded and fiddled with his tablet. "Why you don't, you know, go to the police?"

Connie said, "We're working with them, Javier. That Detective Amelia. She knows who we are. She's just keeping up the cover when she called us the Abbotts."

Morales nodded. "Remember what she asked you? Where you and your father were yesterday? That's what we're trying to find out. How're you coming with the pictures?"

"I couldn't remember very much."

Morales had looked at the tablet earlier. The boy had done some cartoon sketches but none related to the redheaded cop's assignment.

Morales said, "My associate here, Mr. Ortiz, has found out almost everywhere he went. Except for an hour about three p.m. Three in the afternoon. Do you know what delivery he made then? If we can figure that out we can figure out who killed him. And catch him."

"Them," the boy said. "You said 'men.'"

"Them." Morales smiled.

But Javier was shaking his head. "I dunno. I was drawing. Just hanging in the truck, you know."

"Think back. At around two thirty he made a delivery at...?" He looked at Ortiz.

"Tony's Auto Supply. It's on Fourteenth and the river."

Morales smiled. "That's near the garbage scows. You remember that? There'd be seagulls. Thousands of seagulls. And the place stinks too."

His eyes narrowed. "Yeah. Birds. All those birds. There, yeah."

Morales's wife, Connie, pointed out, "And at three thirty he dropped off something in Chinatown. You know Chinatown."

"Yeah. I 'member that."

"What delivery did he make in between? Around three?"

"Nothing. Didn't drop nothing off."

Morales's face revealed no emotion. He studied the boy closely. He wondered if he was lying and if Coelho should go to work on him. "But it wouldn't take an hour to get from the river to Chinatown. We're sure he made a delivery."

"No." Then stridently: "He didn't."

Morales sighed. "So he didn't stop *anywhere*?"

"Sure, we stopped. But he didn't deliver anything. You asked me if he delivered something and he didn't."

Morales laughed. The kid was right. He'd been asking the wrong question. "Where did he stop?"

"The church."

"Church?"

"Yeah. After the place with all the birds we drove for a while and he went into this church and then we left and drove to Chinatown."

"Church? Was your dad religious?" Coelho asked.

"Huh?" The boy was frowning.

"Did he go to church Sundays, to mass?"

"No. That's why I thought it was, you know, weird."

"Can you show us where the church is?"

"I guess. Only, can I get my paper and pencils?"

"We don't have time to worry about that now," Coelho snapped.

"My daddy gave them to me," the boy said defiantly.

Morales smiled. "Sure, son." And Connie climbed the stairs to fetch the set.

* * *

Getting away from the building without being seen was the hardest part: Up to the roof, over three buildings then down again.

Morales was worried that the boy would freak out at the heights, and cry out in fear, even if they weren't near the edge. But, no, he was fine, though he was upset when they told him that Officer Lamont, the bodyguard, was actually working for the men who'd killed his father and they couldn't trust him.

Morales was feeling a little bad that he'd have to kill the kid as soon as they got their hands on the delivery. That was one hit he wouldn't do himself. Stan Coelho would. The ATF agent would ice anyone, any age, any sex. He suspected the man was psycho. Though that condition had come in helpful from time to time.

Once on the street, and nowhere near the surveilling cop, the five of them slipped into Connie's Lexis SUV and headed off, downtown.

Javier told them that he could not remember exactly where the church was, but once they arrived in the vicinity of Chinatown and started driving in lazy circles it took only ten minutes for the boy to sit up and cry out, "There!" He pointed excitedly to St. Timothy's, a grimy gothic Catholic church near the Bowery.

Ortiz and Connie smiled, but Morales shook his head as he eyed the place carefully. It was small and without a back entrance or loading dock.

There was a service door but in the front; you reached it via the main sidewalk, which was crowded now and would have been just as congested when Rinaldo had been here, around three yesterday afternoon.

Morales muttered, "How could he get two tons of... product through the door and not be seen?"

It was then that Ortiz laughed. "What if he wasn't going to hide the shipment itself?"

"What do you mean?"

"You were nervous about a sting or surveillance. Maybe he was too. He meets the truck in the armory, tries out a product or two, makes sure they're all there. But he's worried and wants some escape plan. So he's arranged for the guy who picked up the shipment at the Jersey train depot to keep it and take it to, I don't know, a self-storage unit somewhere."

Morales was nodding. Smart. It was a smart plan.

Connie added, "He writes down the details, the address of the storage place and combination to the lock, in the church. *That's* what he hides here." A nod at the church.

Morales had to laugh. He looked at the boy. "Your papa knew what he was about."

"Unless," Stan Coelho was saying, "it's a red herring."

"How so?"

"Just trying to lead off anybody following him."

Morales noticed the agent's eyes were on the boy's pencil box.

Coelho asked, "Where'd you get that?"

"It's mine," he said defiantly.

"I didn't ask that. I want to know where you got it."

"My daddy gave it to me."

"When?"

"Yesterday."

"Shit, *that's* got the information in it. The storage space. Probably the key. He's had it all along." He reached for it.

"Mine!" Javier cried. "There's no key in it." The boy pulled away. "My daddy had one but he didn't give it to me."

Morales waved his hand and Coelho backed off. "Your daddy had one what?"

"A key."

"Where did he get it?"

"When we stopped here, he took it out of the glove compartment thing, you know. And he took it into the church."

"You know where he put it?"

"No. I stayed here and drawed. Came back just a minute later and we drove off, to Chinatown."

Morales said, "Let's go. We'll all go to look." They climbed out of the SUV and headed for the church. Coelho kept his hand on Javier's shoulder. If the key wasn't here, Morales would tell the agent to go to work and get the boy to talk. He couldn't afford to waste any more time.

Inside, the dark church was largely deserted, only a few worshipers were present, scattered around the space, lost in prayer or contemplation. Morales was wondering how to search for the key and not make anyone suspicious. But then he realized that Rinaldo would have thought of this; he'd hide the key in a place that was easy to get to naturally.

Not the holy water font. Not the altar. Even under a pew or kneeler would have been too risky; an exploring child might find it, or a parishioner who dropped a wallet or coin.

Ah, but then he saw what might be the answer.

A votive candle rack.

No unsupervised children. And no one would think twice about someone reaching into the rack to light a candle to the Lord or the Virgin.

He told the others his theory, and he, Ortiz and his wife approached the three racks — one in front of a statue of Jesus, one before Mary, and one in front of a simple cross.

Coelho stayed with the child. Morales got the impression he was already anticipating, with some pleasure, killing the boy.

Morales found nothing under his rack. Ortiz too came up empty handed. But as he looked across the pews he noticed his wife nodding and smiling. Something small and silver disappeared into her pocket.

He inhaled deeply and, in thanks, lit a candle himself. And slipped a hundred dollar offering in the box chained to a radiator by the door.

As the entourage left the church, Connie whispered to him. "Saf-Storage in Queens. He even wrote the address."

Morales whispered, "We'll get somebody over there now. And I want to go back to the Abbotts and wait for that cop, the woman, Sachs. Take her out and the bodyguard too."

Connie said absently "She had such nice hair. Didn't you think?"

Morales said nothing. He was then vaguely aware of some people walking behind them, presumably the parishioners who'd left, though he hadn't seen any of them stand and head out the door.

They were just at the SUV when it happened.

From behind him came a woman's voice, sternly shouting: "Police! Hands where we can see them! Get down on your knees! Now, now, now!"

A dozen tactical police officers appeared from hiding places between parked cars in front of the church, and four squad cars and three unmarkeds skidded to a stop around them.

Connie screamed and flung her hands in the air. Ortiz, who'd been arrested several times, knew he'd end up on the ground eventually and simply flopped onto his belly, hands outstretched. Morales sighed and lifted his hands. He turned to see the woman whose death he'd just been planning — Detective Sachs — leading the tactical operation. He gave a faint laugh, observing that all of the cops wore two bullet-proof vests, and he realized that, since they knew about the special armor-piercing bullets, they probably knew everything.

His whole plan, so brilliant, in ruins.

"Now!" Detective Sachs shouted.

Morales turned to his wife. "Do what they say. Get on your knees."

"My stockings, my shoes!"

"Go ahead," he said kindly. "And don't do anything quickly. You'll be all right."

Then the redhead was shouting, "You, Coelho! Let go of the boy. On the ground. Now!"

Morales glanced back. And saw the ATF agent, angry resolve in his fat face, looking about. Suddenly he gripped the boy by the chest and lifted him, drawing his gun and aiming it toward the police, who scattered for cover. The redhead stayed where she was, but crouched, trying to find a target. But Javier was not a tiny boy and he proved to be a decent human shield, despite the agent's girth.

"Coelho," she said. "You know the drill. You'll never get out of here. Put the weapon down."

"Have the woman throw me the key to the Lexus. Now!"

"No," Detective Sachs said. "It won't happen."

"Then I'll kill the boy." He tapped Javier's forehead with the gun.

Morales said, "No, Stan. Let him go!" He in truth didn't care about the boy's safety, but if Coelho killed him, it would be another count of homicide — felony murder — against all of those present, even if not directly involved in Javier's death.

But the agent ignored him.

"Keys! I'm not asking again."

The policewoman: "You shoot him, you die one second later."

"Keys," he roared.

"No."

Suddenly a huge crack of gunshot and the pistol in Coelho's hand jumped.

Morales's wife cried out and even the redheaded cop, so cool a moment ago, gasped in horror.

Morales, not daring to move much, craned his neck further around so he could see Coelho and the boy. Javier was slipping through the big man's arms to the ground.

The pistol fell from Coelho's grip and he looked down at a blossoming red wound in his own chest.

"I... I... "

The gunshot, Morales noted, hadn't come from the agent's Glock. The gun had merely jerked as Coelho had reacted. No, it had been *Javier* who'd fired. He looked at the boy, who was holding a very small pistol in his hand. On the ground was his pencil box, unzipped. Pencils had fallen out, a pencil sharpener, too. And so had another magazine of ammunition for the weapon.

A present from his father…

The redheaded officer walked slowly to the boy and whispered something Morales could not hear. Javier nodded and handed her the gun, while a dozen other cops got to Coelho, pulled him down and secured his weapon. A medic appeared a moment later and began administering first aid.

Officers descended on Connie and Morales, cuffing and frisking. They began reading Miranda rights. Detective Sachs joined them a moment later and began reciting a laundry list of what they were being arrested for.

The litany went on for some time.

***

The answer to uncovering Morales's deception, fronting that he and his wife were the Abbotts, derived, Rhyme regretted admitting, not so much from finely parsed evidence but from a good old-fashioned street detective's deduction.

Rhyme was at his computer, writing up the report on the case for the NYPD, the FBI and the ATFE, who would be running the joint prosecution against Morales, his wife, Constance, Raphael Ortiz and the wounded, but very much alive, Stan Coelho, as well as assorted associates in the 128 Lords.

Rhyme's deduction had been this: When Sachs had called Javier to ask if he'd been with his father at the armory when the transfer took place yesterday morning, the woman purporting to be Sally Abbott, the temporary foster parent, had helped clarify the location of the armory; the boy wasn't sure what Sachs was referring to.

But in describing the armory to Javier, she referred to McDonald's — which was across the street from the *back* entrance of the armory, a small service portal, not the main doorways on the opposite side of the building a block away. Why would that entrance be first in her thoughts to describe the place?

The implication was that she'd known Echi Rinaldo used that door to get inside.

It wasn't conclusive proof that Sally Abbott knew about the delivery. But it raised in Rhyme's mind the possibility that he — and therefore his wife — were not who they seemed to be. Sachs got pictures of the Abbotts from the foster family licensing organization and confirmed that they were not the people she'd left the boy with.

They immediately sent a tactical and surveillance team to the town house — just in time to see the couple, along with several other men and the boy, fleeing over the roof.

Rhyme and Sachs reasoned that it was likely they were taking the boy to lead them to the arms stash and so the surveillance officers followed, while a tactical team secured the town house... and made the unfortunate but not unexpected discovery of the Abbotts' bodies, in the basement.

When they'd arrived at the church — probably the site of the weapons, or some lead to send them to the stash, Sachs joined the team for the takedown, ready to move in the minute the boy appeared in danger, even if they didn't find the weapons. But, as it turned out, Javier didn't need as much protection as they'd thought. (Sachs grimaced at the thought that she had missed the LCP .380 pocket gun he'd carried in his pencil box — though, true, he'd been in the company of police at his father's murder scene and then with Child Protective Services personnel; she assumed he'd been properly searched.)

The ATF now had possession of the weapons — five hundred of some of the most sophisticated submachine guns on earth. Street value of three-quarters of a million. And the Mexican police had seized a large factory in Chihuahua, "Juarez-Trenton Exhaust Systems," which produced not a single emissions control device but had quite the sophisticated operation, from computer design to stringent quality control. Several trucking company officials were also in custody. More arrests were expected.

As Rhyme put the finishing touches on his report, he was interrupted. A figure appeared in the doorway. "Damn, you were gonna come watch but you missed it."

Rhyme grumbled, "I missed it."

"You didn't see it?"

"No, like I said. I missed it. What exactly?"

"A goal! 'Nother one. A header... " He pointed to Rhyme. "Yo, Mr. Rhyme, *you* could hit headers! Don't need your legs for that!"

Indisputable, Rhyme reflected, looking over at the boy.

Javier and Thom had been in the music room across the hall, presently playing the soccer game — on, no less, Rhyme's biggest and most expensive high-def monitor, wheeled from lab to den for the purpose of lowly amusement.

"It was unfair," called Thom Reston, representing Brazil. "We're down three-nil." Javier was Mexico.

"What's unfair?" Rhyme called to his unseen aide.

"Well, he's younger. He's more agile."

"It's a video game," Rhyme reminded.

"Thumbs require agility too."

Javier returned to the match. "You gotta come watch!"

"All right." He saved his document and wheeled into the den, where, in concession for being a spectator, he was given a slug of single-malt by Thom, before returning to the game.

Rhyme sipped, Rhyme watched.

The boy would be staying here tonight. Child and Family Services had finally tracked down the aunt, in Chicago. She would be arriving to take him to her suburban home tomorrow. She was married, Sachs had reported, and had two children of her own.

Rhyme actually cheered the boy on, drawing a scowl from Thom.

Twenty minutes later Sachs arrived and he wheeled from the digital stadium and joined her in the parlor lab.

She'd been interviewing the suspects in the case — Morales and his wife kept mum but Ortiz and Stan Coelho were happy to talk, though some of the latter's willingness to spill may have been due to happy drugs.

"None of them can think of who might've killed him." She nodded at the evidence table, meaning Rinaldo. Morales, his wife and the other two minders, of course, weren't prime suspects; the success of their arms importing scheme depended on a living deliveryman.

"Somebody within the 128s? A rival crew? A contractor who just happened to hear about the guns and wanted to steal the shipment?"

She shrugged. And even as he'd asked the question he'd decided such perps were unlikely. No, his and Sachs's first conclusion somehow smelled right: that Rinaldo's was a random death, unrelated to the arms scheme.

Wrong time, wrong place.

These were, he knew, the hardest homicides to close.

"Well, we've still got the evidence. A mountain's worth of it." He glanced at the tables. "The answer's there someplace."

"I'll call Mel in and we'll get to it."

At that moment Rhyme's computer sounded with an incoming email. He glanced up and read the message. It was from the assistant district attorney he'd worked with from time to time — the one, in fact, who'd run the Baxter case, which had concluded in a guilty verdict against the scam artist, just a few days ago, Rhyme's first foray into white collar crime.

A second email arrive a moment later. From the office of the chief of detectives.

Curious.

He was aware of Sachs looking his way, her head cocking.

"Is something wrong?"

"The ADA and some NYPD brass. They want to meet with me. Today. Something about the Baxter case."

"What do you think it's about, Lincoln?" she asked.

Then her voice braked to a stop. He looked her way. She'd just broken their unspoken but immutable rule. That it was the worst kind of bad luck to use first names when addressing each other. Rhyme had no more use for superstition than he had for sentiment and reverence, but it was a jarring moment.

Still, he smiled. "No clue what's up. Maybe I'm getting a good citizen award." He turned to summon Thom to bring the disabled-accessible van around but he heard young Javier Rinaldo's laugh and Thom mournful cry of "No way, not again!"

Rhyme wheeled toward the den.

City hall could wait.

About the Author

A former journalist, folksinger and attorney, Jeffery Deaver is an international number-one bestselling author. His novels have appeared on bestseller lists around the world, including the *New York Times*, *The Times* of London, Italy's *Corriere della Sera*, the *Sydney Morning Herald* and the *Los Angeles Times*. His books are sold in 150 countries and translated into twenty-five languages.

The author of thirty-seven novels, three collections of short stories and a nonfiction law book, and a lyricist of a country-western album, he's received or been shortlisted for dozens of awards. His *The Bodies Left Behind* was named Novel of the Year by the International Thriller Writers association, and his Lincoln Rhyme thriller *The Broken Window* and a stand-alone, *Edge*, were also nominated for that prize. He has been awarded the Steel Dagger and the Short Story Dagger from the British Crime Writers' Association and the Nero Award, and he is a three-time recipient of the Ellery Queen Readers Award for Best Short Story of the Year and a winner of the British Thumping Good Read Award. *The Cold Moon* was recently named the Book of the Year by the Mystery Writers of Japan, as well as by *Kono Mystery ga Sugoi* magazine. In addition, the Japanese Adventure Fiction Association awarded *The Cold Moon* and *Carte Blanche* their annual Grand Prix award. His book *The Kill Room* was awarded the Political Thriller of the Year by Killer Nashville. And his collection of short stories, *Trouble in Mind*, was nominated for best anthology by that organization, as well.

Deaver has been honored with the Lifetime Achievement Award by the Bouchercon World Mystery Convention and by the Raymond Chandler Lifetime Achievement Award in Italy.

He contributed to the anthology *Books to Die For*, which won the Agatha Award and the Anthony.

His most recent novels are *Solitude Creek*, a Kathryn Dance novel; *The October List*, a thriller told in reverse; *The Skin Collector* and *The Kill Room*, Lincoln Rhyme novels. For his Dance novel *XO* Deaver wrote an album of country-western songs, available on iTunes and as a CD; and before that, *Carte Blanche*, a James Bond continuation novel, a number-one international bestseller.

Deaver has been nominated for seven Edgar Awards from the Mystery Writers of America, an Anthony, a Shamus and a Gumshoe. He was recently shortlisted for the ITV3 Crime Thriller Award for Best International Author. *Roadside Crosses* was on the shortlist for the Prix Polar International 2013.

His book *A Maiden's Grave* was made into an HBO movie starring James Garner and Marlee Matlin, and his novel *The Bone Collector* was a feature release from Universal Pictures, starring Denzel Washington and Angelina Jolie. Lifetime aired an adaptation of his *The Devil's Teardrop*. And, yes, the rumors are true; he did appear as a corrupt reporter on his favorite soap opera, *As the World Turns*. He was born outside Chicago and has a bachelor of journalism degree from the University of Missouri and a law degree from Fordham University.

Readers can visit his website at www.jefferydeaver.com.

Made in the USA
Middletown, DE
05 June 2016